THIS BOOK BELONGS TO:

_____

First published in Great Britain in 2002 by Andersen Press Ltd.,

20 Vauxhall Bridge Road, London SW1V 2SA.

This paperback edition first published in 2010 by Andersen Press Ltd.

Published in Australia by Random House Australia Pty.,

Level 3, 100 Pacific Highway, North Sydney, NSW 2060.

Copyright © Michael Foreman, 2002

Printed and bound in Singapore by Tien Wah Press.

10   9   8   7   6   5   4   3   2   1

British Library Cataloguing in Publication Data available.

ISBN 978 1 84939 047 7

This book has been printed on acid-free paper

DINOSAUR TIME

MICHAEL FOREMAN

ANDERSEN PRESS

It all started at breakfast with the Timer. The new Timer that Tom's mum had bought for the kitchen.

It looked a bit like a flying saucer and it was magnetic.

"This is not a toy," said his mum, sticking it on the fridge. "Don't mess with it."
Then she went next door to talk to old Mrs Cole.

The Timer fitted perfectly in
the palm of Tom's hand.
The blue light winked at him.
He pressed it and the
numbers began to whirr, and
whiz round.

Then the kitchen began to
whiz – round and round,
faster and faster, until the
walls were just a blur. The
noise was tremendous, like
being in the centre of a
giant storm. Everything
flashed from light to dark,
and dark to light . . .

. . . like a million days and
a million nights.

Then, suddenly, all was still
and quiet.

The kitchen, the house, the
street, the town had whizzed
away, leaving Tom standing
in deep grass, by the waters
of a dark lake.

Shadows flickered across
the surface of the water,
and the sky filled with flying
creatures, all toothy and scaly
and all looking at him
with angry eyes.

He turned and ran . . .

. . . and fell –

SMASH!

– into a pit full of eggs
and baby monsters.

The mother dinosaur glared at him.

Perhaps he should have said, "Sorry," but he just ran, with the baby dinosaurs following and snapping at his heels.

The mother dinosaur chased after them . . . and even bigger dinosaurs joined in.

When he reached the edge of a huge precipice, Tom remembered his mum's warning. If only he hadn't messed with that Timer, like she said . . .

Of course! The Timer! It was still in his pocket. The little blue light winked at him. He pressed it.

The roaring
dinosaurs,
with their gaping
jaws and rows
of teeth, whizzed
round him,
round and round,
faster and faster.

A million days and a million nights flashed and stormed around his ears, then stopped . . .

The Timer in Tom's hand stopped whirring. In his other hand was an egg, with a crack in it.
It was warm and gently throbbing.

He was back in the kitchen.
He heard his Mum say, "Bye-bye, Mrs Cole," and open the back door.

In a panic, he put the egg in a bucket in the broom cupboard and covered it with a towel. His mum came in and put the kettle on. Then his dad came home and they had supper.

In the middle of the night, Tom crept downstairs and looked in the broom cupboard. The egg wasn't there, but its contents were – all scaly and toothy.

But it didn't look fierce. Just sad.

It seemed to be getting bigger all the time. And the bigger it got the sadder it looked. "You can't stay here," said Tom. "I'm sorry, but you've got to go back."

It was heavy and stuck fast
in the bucket, but Tom
could just lift it.
When he got it into the
garden, he fixed the Timer
to the side of the bucket and
kissed the little dinosaur on
the nose.

Then he pressed the blue
button . . .

It was like a whirlwind.

Whizz!

BANG!

Gone.

All that was left was a round mark in the grass made by the bottom of the bucket.

Tom hoped the little dinosaur would get home safely . . .

. . . but what was he going to tell his mum about the Timer?

And as far away as a million nights and a million days, a mother dinosaur said to her son . . .

"This is not a toy. Don't mess with it."

"No, Mum," said the little dinosaur . . .

But the blue button was winking at him.